D0470794

Jackson
County
Library
System

The Little Hills of Nazareth

Bijou Le Tord

BRADBURY PRESS   NEW YORK

Bradbury Press
An Affiliate of Macmillan, Inc.
866 Third Avenue, New York, NY 10022
Collier Macmillan Canada, Inc.
10 9 8 7 6 5 4 3 2 1

The text of this book is set in Zapf International.
The illustrations are watercolor.

Printed and bound in Japan

LIBRARY OF CONGRESS CATALOGING-IN-PUBLICATION DATA

Le Tord, Bijou.
The little hills of Nazareth.

Summary: Naboth the donkey was a companion to
Joseph and Mary and was in the stable with them the
night of Jesus's birth.
[1. Jesus Christ—Nativity—Fiction.   2. Donkeys—
Fiction]   I. Title.
PZ7.L568Lh   1988   [E]   86-32657
ISBN 0-02-756480-0

FOR MAYA

And all the trees
of the field shall
clap their hands.

Isaiah 55:12

God
created

Joseph and
Mary.

He also
created

Naboth
to be their
companion.

Joseph was kind.

He gave
wheat to
Naboth.

He
picked
apricots

for
their
supper.

God
loved Mary

and

Joseph.

Mary
would bake
bread

for Joseph,
herself, and
Naboth.

Every day she
would walk over
the hills to
fetch water

for
their
supper.

When it came
time for
Mary

to give
birth,

Joseph took
her to
Bethlehem

where
she rested
in a small
stable

between Joseph
and Naboth.

In the
deep of the
night

a little
babe
cried.

Jesus was born.

And in the
hills nearby
shepherds
rejoiced.

There was
music and
it said:
*"Praise be
to God."*

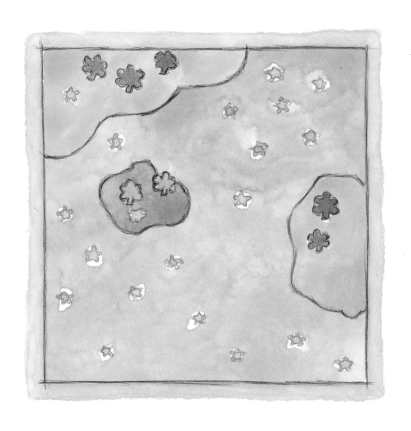

And the
stars
illuminated

the Sea of
Galilee.

Everywhere
you could see
and feel
the love of God

for all mankind
and all creatures,

like Naboth,
His little
donkey.